Yes, A Cat Named Marty Cohen

WENDY ANN GARDNER

HYPERION
BOOKS FOR
CHILDREN
NEW YORK

TEXT AND ILLUSTRATIONS © 2002 BY WENDY ANN GARDNER

BOOK DESIGN BY POLLY KANEVSKY

First Edition

1 3 5 7 9 10 8 6 4 2

ISBN 0-7868-0887-X

Library of Congress Catalog Card Number on file.

Printed in Singapore

Visit www.hyperionchildrensbooks.com
and www.scarystories.com

For Fabian

In a land so far away,

where thistles grow, and skies are gray,

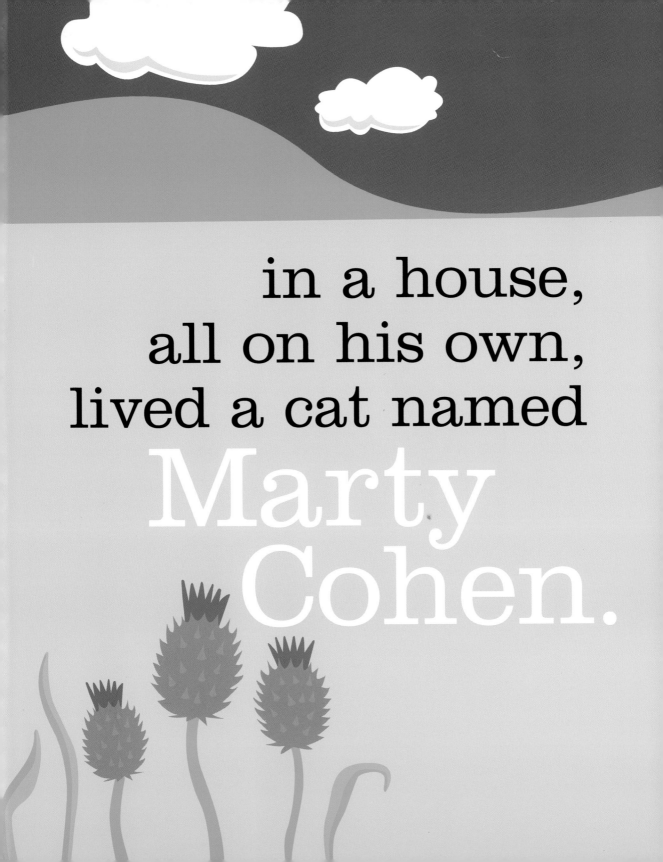

in a house,
all on his own,
lived a cat named
Marty
Cohen.

Although
by all
he was
adored,

he found
himself
a little

bored.

So he
thought
he'd take a trip,
get aboard a
great big
ship,

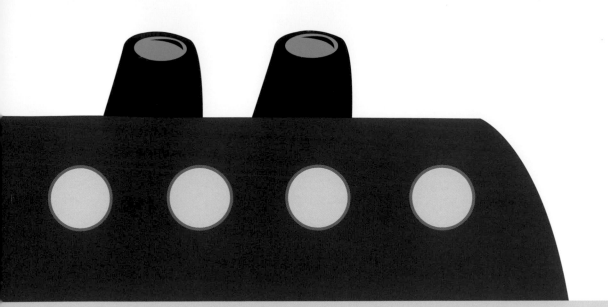

and **sail**
across the
choppy
sea

in
search
of his
destiny.

With that thought
he took a
chance,
packed his shirt,
packed his pants,

his
favorite
things

SALTINES

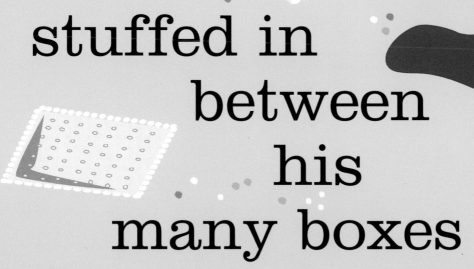

stuffed in
between
his
many boxes

of Saltines.

After
several
days
went by
of seeing
only
sea and sky,

he wondered if
he'd ever find
more
than what
he'd left
behind.

Then, at last,
a celebration—
he'd reached his
sunny
destination.

Now
his trip
had
finally
ended—

Scotland

off he went to be
befriended.

"I'm from Scotland," said Marty, "but this is where I want to be!"

Happy
now
in his
new home—
yes, a cat
named
Marty
Cohen.